First published in Great Britain in 2017 by Hodder and Stoughton

Hodder Children's Books
An imprint of Hachette Children's Group
Part of Hodder and Stoughton
Carmelite House
50 Victoria Embankment
London EC4Y 0DZ

ISBN 978 1 444 92785 6
Printed in China

An Hachette UK Company
www.hachette.co.uk

Hodder
Children's
Books

Thank You,
Mr Panda

Steve Antony

Who are all
the presents
for, Mr Panda?

My friends.

This is for Mouse.

A present for me, Mr Panda?

It's the thought
that counts.

But it's
too big.

A gift for me,
Mr Panda?

But I have eight legs.

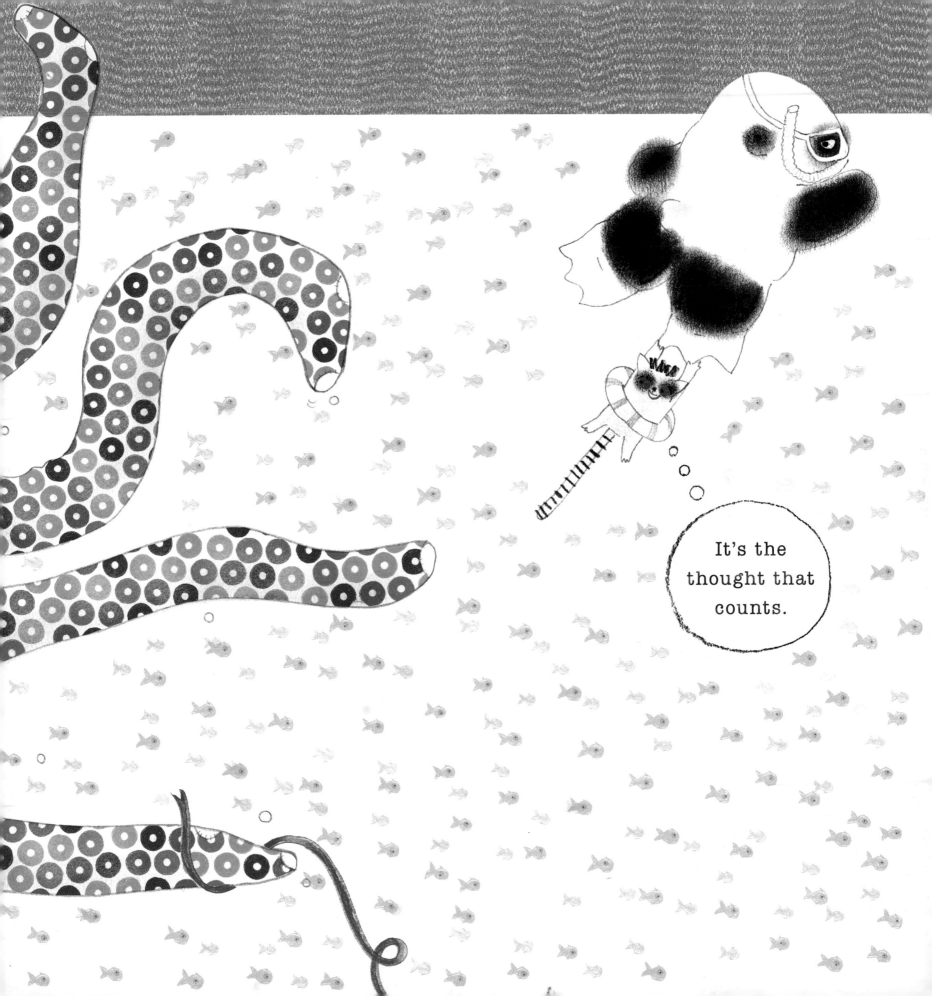

It's the thought that counts.

This is for Elephant.

I will open it later.

And this is for
Mountain Goat.

Something for me, Mr Panda?

But it's too heavy.

It's the thought that counts.

Who is the
last present
for, Mr Panda?

It's for you.

Thank you, Mr Panda!

You're welcome,
but remember...

...it's the thought that counts.